Yan's Hajj
The Journey of a Lifetime

D1511976

THE ISLAMIC FOUNDATION

For a man my father loved, whose beautiful Fajr reminders have resonated in the Rutter Street Mosque for decades. Dr. Mohammed Siddiq is the kindest and gentlest soul I know. I love you, Uncle.

Yan's Hajj

First Published in 2018 by
THE ISLAMIC FOUNDATION

Distributed by
KUBE PUBLISHING LTD
Tel +44 (0)1530 249230, Fax +44 (0)1530 249656
E-mail: info@kubepublishing.com
Website: www.kubepublishing.com

Author: Fawzia Gilani
Illustrator: Sophie Burrows
Book design: Rebecca Wildman

A Cataloguing-in-Publication Data record for this book is available from the British Library

ISBN 978-0-86037-623-1

Printed in Istanbul, Turkey by IMAK Ofset

Yan's Hajj
The Journey of a Lifetime

by
FAWZIA GILANI

Illustrated by
SOPHIE BURROWS

Once upon a time there lived a kind and happy farmer named Yan, who loved Allah more than anything else. His dream was to visit the Kaaba, Allah's house, and do Hajj.

The problem was – he was poor. And he would need to fill his money bag first.

After some years of hard work Yan's money bag was full. He could go to Makkah. Soon his dream would come true.

As he took the first steps of his journey he looked up at the sky and said, "I love you Allah!"

After days of walking, Yan had crossed the mountains. There he saw a group of children sitting on the ground. They looked sad. "Children, why do you look so sad? And why aren't you at school?" Yan said.

"Our school burned down and we don't have any money to fix it," they replied.

Yan smiled. "I have some money. Inshallah I will fix your school."

6

Yan set to work on the school.
He repaired the leaky roof.

He replaced the broken windows.

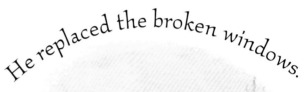

And he rebuilt the crumbling walls.

S oon the school was ready.
The children were overjoyed and thanked Yan for his kindness.

But when Yan looked in his bag,
all his Hajj money
was gone.

Yan went back to his farm and prayed to Allah,
"I will work hard, save my money and inshallah I will do Hajj."

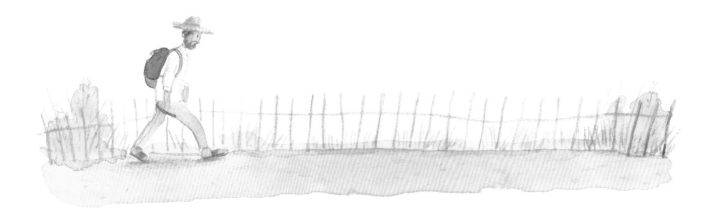

Back on the farm many years went by. Yan worked hard caring for his crops and saved as much as he could. Until one day, his money bag was full.

"Alhamdulillah, praise be to Allah," said Yan. "Now I can go and do Hajj."

Yan picked up his money bag and got on his horse.

Yan had not ridden far when he saw a small boy beside the road.
The boy was holding his leg and looked in pain. Yan ran over.

Suddenly, a big man appeared. He stood over the boy. "Get up. You must work!" he yelled. "But the boy is hurt," said Yan.

"The boy must work! He owes me lots of money," the man replied. Yan took his Hajj money and gave it to the man. After a grunt and a glance at the coins, the man walked away. The boy was free to leave.

The boy looked at Yan and said, "I have nowhere to go and I cannot walk." "Don't worry," smiled Yan, "I will care for you until you are strong."

So Habeeb, as the boy was called, went to live with Yan on his farm.

13

Habeeb grew strong as he got older. Soon he was able to help Yan catch the chickens and look after the animals.

Yet, despite how much Habeeb loved Yan, sometimes he would wonder about his family. One afternoon Habeeb said to Yan, "I miss my parents. I want to find my mum and dad."
Yan nodded and smiled. "Yes, of course," he said, "you must go and find them so you can be happy."

Not long after Habeeb set out to find his family.

ithout Habeeb, life on the farm was hard for Yan.
But his dream to do Hajj gave him strength.

One day when Yan looked at his money bag, it was full.
"Alhamdulillah," said Yan, "Now I can go and do Hajj."

Yan was old now so he sat in
a cart which his horse pulled
along the path.

On his way Yan stopped at a village. A group of people were talking together. They wanted to build a mosque but they did not have enough money. They were sad.

"Don't be sad," said Yan. "I will help you build a mosque. I have some money."

Yan carried bricks and stones. He hammered nails and cut tiles.
Yan worked hard with the villagers.
After two months the mosque was complete.

hen Yan looked in his money bag all his Hajj money was gone. So Yan went back to his farm.

On the journey home he looked up at the sky. "Dear Allah," he said, "I will work hard and save my money. One day I will do Hajj."

But Yan was old now and he could not work fast.
The next time Yan looked in his money bag; it was not full.
"I cannot do Hajj," he said sadly.

Later that day, Yan saw a man riding a horse towards his farm.
"Who is that?" said Yan, peering through his glasses.

The man came near.
"It's me, Habeeb," he said. "I have
come to take you to do Hajj."

Yan was overjoyed. "Jazakallah Habeeb. We must leave before I get any older!" he said.

Habeeb helped Yan onto the cart. They drove along the dusty path talking together and praising Allah.

S oon they passed a school. The children ran outside waving and smiling. They shouted, "We love you." They threw rose petals on him and gave him white sheets to wear on Hajj.

Many days later they passed through a village.

When the people saw Yan they ran out from
their homes and the mosque to greet him.
They gave Yan gifts of food and water and
said, "We love you Yan."

25

Some weeks passed and Habeeb stopped the cart outside a small house. A man and woman stood outside.

"Thank you for taking care of our son," said the man and woman. They gave Yan a bag filled with money.

"We love you!" they said.

And soon after...

... Yan arrived in Makkah.
Habeeb took Yan to the Kaaba.
Yan smiled and tears came to his eyes.
He looked up at the sky and said, "I love You, Allah!"

Yan's dream had
finally come true.

Other children's books by Fawzia Gilani

Cinderella: An Islamic Tale
9780860374732

Snow White: An Islamic Tale
9780860375265

Husna and the Eid Party: An Eid Story
9780860374060

The Lost Ring
9780860375654